The Ghost Train

ALLAN AHLBERG · ANDRE AMSTUTZ

HEINEMANN · LONDON

William Heinemann Ltd
Michelin House
81 Fulham Road, London SW3 6RB
First published 1992
ISBN 0434 96084 5
Printed in Hong Kong

On a dark dark hill
there is a dark dark town.
In the dark dark town
there is a dark dark street.
Down the dark dark street
there is a dark dark station.
And in the dark dark station . . .

there is a ghost train!

Whooooooo!

One night, the big skeleton,
the little skeleton
and the dog skeleton
go for a ride on the ghost train.

They leave the dark dark cellar
and walk down the dark dark street.
They peep in at a few windows
on the way.

"How peaceful!" says the big skeleton.
"How nice!" the little skeleton says.

At the station
they get their tickets
from a monster
and have them punched
by another monster.
"How helpful!" says the big skeleton.
"How kind!" the little skeleton says.

At midnight, the ghost train arrives.
"Do you believe in ghosts?"
says the ghost.
"Yes!" the skeletons say.
"Good," says the ghost.
"Climb aboard!"

And off they go –
out of the dark dark station,
out of the dark dark town,
up and over the dark dark hill
and into the dark dark night.

The three skeletons
sit next to a big monster
and share a joke
with a little monster.
"How friendly!" says the big skeleton.
"What fun!" the little skeleton says.

At one o'clock the train arrives
at Ghost-Town-by-the-Sea.

The skeletons leave the train
and stroll around.
They kick the ghost of a ball
and catch the ghost of a fish.
They paddle in the dark dark sea
and ride on the dark dark donkeys.

THE MONSTERS' BEAUTY PARADE.

"How charming!" says the big skeleton.
"What glamour!" the little skeleton says.

At three o'clock
the ghost train whistle blows.
It is time to leave.
The skeletons climb aboard
and off they go –
away from the dark dark sea,
away from the dark dark sand,
in and out of the very dark dark tunnel
and into the dark dark night.

At four o'clock
the train arrives at the station.

The big skeleton, the little skeleton
and the dog skeleton hurry home.
They peep in at a few windows
on the way.
Suddenly, a <u>baby</u> cries.
(Do you believe in babies?)
"Waaaaa!"

Waaaaa!

"How frightful!" says the big skeleton.
"How scary!" the little skeleton says.
"How—l!" howls the dog.

And off they run —
into the house,
down the stairs,
into the cellar
and <u>under</u> the bed.

On a dark dark hill
there is a dark dark town.
In the dark dark town
there is a dark dark street.
Down the dark dark street
there is a dark dark station.
And in the dark dark station
there is a ghost train.

The End